D0310975

Who is the first passenger?

Someone very special is waiting at the Magic Roundabout.

Who's waiting for the train behind the trees?

What's that, Mr MacHenry?

Now, who's that in the end carriage?

Who's already eating? We're almost ready for the picnic!

Mr MacHenry's
Super Vegetable
Plot

Time for the picnic at last.

But there's someone who can help.

That's better.
"Thank you, Zebedee," says everyone.

What a lovely day!